Ms. Wilde
and Oscar

Lee Aucoin, *Creative Director*
Jamey Acosta, *Senior Editor*
Heidi Fiedler, *Editor*
Produced and designed by
Denise Ryan & Associates
Illustration © Sarah Hornel
Rachelle Cracchiolo, *Publisher*

Teacher Created Materials
5301 Oceanus Drive
Huntington Beach, CA 92649-1030
http://www.tcmpub.com
Paperback: ISBN: 978-1-4333-5611-7
Library Binding: ISBN: 978-1-4807-1733-6
© 2014 Teacher Created Materials

Written by
Sharon Callen

Illustrated by
Sarah Hornel

Contents

Chapter One

Ms. Wilde
and
Oscar

Ms. Wilde was the most interesting teacher in the whole wide world.

On the first day of school, she came dressed as Snow White. She told her class the whole story as she acted it out. The next day, she came dressed as Robin Hood. She acted out that story, too. She came dressed as a different storybook character every day. But that's not all that made her interesting.

Ms. Wilde brought her dog with her to school every day. She called him her "little helper." He had big, round eyes, short little legs, a fluffy, round body, and a perky little tail. His name was Oscar. Every day he came to school dressed in costume, too.

SNOW
White

5

The whole class loved listening to Ms. Wilde's stories. They loved watching her and Oscar act them out. She told funny stories, sad stories, stories about faraway places, and stories about wonderful characters. Soon, all the children were begging Ms. Wilde to let them tell stories, dress up, and act them out.

One day, Ms. Wilde announced they would do exactly that. She tapped a plan out on her laptop. "First, we will decide on the stories to tell and the characters you will play. Second, we will order costumes. Third, we will have a performance. And, fourth, we will *all* be stars!"

Chapter Two

Checking the Tally

The class began planning. By the end of the lesson, everyone in the class wanted to tell the story of Little Red Riding Hood.

But the story only had five characters. Everyone wanted a speaking part. Everyone wanted to wear a costume. Oscar curled up in his basket while Ms. Wilde tried to help the class find a solution.

"We have thirty students in our class. Why don't we have six groups of five tell the story of Little Red Riding Hood? Then, you can each have the part you want," Ms. Wilde suggested.

The children liked that idea. They organized themselves into groups, so everyone got the part they wanted. Everyone was happy. Oscar stayed curled up in his basket. He wasn't happy.

The next day, Ms. Wilde said she would be ordering the costumes for the performance. "First, we must count all the costumes we need for each character. We need to get this right, or our plays will be a disaster," Ms. Wilde said.

The students made a tally chart on the board. After they finished the tally chart, Ms. Wilde looked at the class and said, "We need to double-check our tallies." Well, they double-checked and triple-checked them!

Ms. Wilde jumped up and clapped her hands. "We are ready to order our costumes!" she rejoiced. The whole class jumped up and clapped their hands with excitement, too.

Oscar kept on sleeping. He hadn't moved all day.

Chapter Three

Oscar Interferes

After school, Ms. Wilde used her laptop to order the costumes from her favorite online store. She had almost finished when the principal knocked on her door.

"Ms. Wilde, did you forget we have a meeting this afternoon?" she asked. "Oh, I'm so sorry, Ms. Douglas! I did forget. I've been so excited about ordering the costumes for the class performance. I'll come down to your office now."

Oscar opened one eye and stared at Ms. Wilde. "Sorry, Oscar," she said. "I forgot about this meeting." She hurried from the classroom.

Oscar was not happy. He was hungry. He looked up and saw Ms. Wilde had left some sunflower seeds on her desk. Oscar loved sunflower seeds. He scrambled out of his basket. He leapt on to Ms. Wilde's chair and jumped on her desk.

Oscar nuzzled the packet of seeds. He nuzzled it just a bit too hard and it fell on the floor! Oscar peered over the edge of the desk. It seemed a long way back down. He looked around and saw Ms. Wilde's open laptop. He nudged it and discovered how warm it was!

And that's when Oscar did something he had never done before. He stood on the laptop. He walked around on the keyboard a few times. And then a few times more. He liked the clicking sound it made under his paws. The computer made a satisfied beep. Then, Oscar curled up and drifted off to sleep, enjoying his nice warm bed.

Chapter Four

The Performance

Oscar heard Ms. Wilde returning. He jumped down from the desk, ate the scattered seeds, and got back into his basket.

Ms. Wilde walked into the room. "Time to go home, Oscar!" she said. As Ms. Wilde and Oscar walked home, Ms. Wilde remembered she hadn't finished ordering the costumes. The minute they arrived home, she checked her laptop.

"Hey, Oscar," she said, "I must be getting forgetful. The order has already been made. I don't even remember doing it."

The children practiced their plays every day and made all the props. On Tuesday afternoon, the office called to let Ms. Wilde know a large box had arrived. When it was delivered to the classroom, all the children knew what was inside.

But as Ms. Wilde opened the box, she realized something had gone *very* wrong with the order. She held up each costume. She looked at the order form. The class gasped! Ms. Wilde sighed. The costumes were all wrong!

"It's OK, Ms. Wilde," said Harry. "We don't mind if we didn't get the right costumes. We'll just tell different stories."

"Yeah," said Mimi. "It was silly that we all wanted to do the same story. The plays will be even better this way!"

The children spent the rest of the day working out new stories to tell with the costumes they had. On Friday, they performed for their parents. The plays were a huge success. Everyone was happy.

Ms. Wilde often wondered about that order. Why had it been such a mess? They had counted so carefully. They had double-checked and triple-checked the order. Maybe she needed a vacation. But one thing was for sure, the performers were all stars!

Sharon Callen lives in Adelaide, Australia. Sharon is a writer, teacher, and literacy consultant who works with children, teachers, and administrators in elementary schools. She spent a number of years working in New York City schools before returning home to Adelaide. Sharon has written many books for the early levels of Read! Explore! Imagine! Fiction Readers as well as *Soo Yun's Book*, *The Curious Café*, *The Happy Faces Leave Home*, and *The Lovely One*.

Sarah Horne lives in London, England. Sarah grew up in a very artistic family, so she was immersed in the world of art and design from the time she was very small. Her illustrations are filled with energy and humor as you will discover in *Ms. Wilde and Oscar,* which is her first book for Read! Explore! Imagine! Fiction Readers.